The Kewtees

For Clare and Pip

**In Memory of John Hilder 1951-2011,
a brilliant illustrator and real gentleman**

The author would like to thank Kew Gardens for their kind permission
to depict the Palm House and Temperate House in this book.

ISBN 978·0·9544751·1·6

Published by Park House Press, 11 Park House Gardens, Twickenham, Middlesex TW1 2DF

www.kewtees.co.uk

The Kewtees

By Colin Hines
Illustrated by John Hilder

Petal

Bud

Aunt Rosa

At Home in the Forest

Kewtees, as you might imagine, live in Kew Gardens. They are tiny, plump, buck-toothed creatures, and the tops of their heads are covered in little green leaves. This allows them to blend in with the Baby's Tears plants in Kew's Temperate Greenhouse, which is now their home.

They didn't always live there, though. They originally came from a land far away across the seas where they were called the Plumptums because of their round bellies. They would roll these against the delicious Baby's Tears plants, squeeze out the sap through holes they had made using their two long front teeth and then eat it.

Their original home was both better and worse than living by the River Thames. Better because it was always warm and the Baby's Tears plants were juicier, but far, far worse because of some cruel creatures called Vampees, who also lived in their forest home. The Vampees hunted them at night and liked nothing better than to eat them!

This is the story of the Kewtees' bravery on their great journey to Kew Gardens.

The Ghastly Vampees

Aunt Rosa was telling her niece Petal and her nephew Bud about life in the old country and particularly about the vicious Vampees. At the mention of the V word, Bud and Petal hugged each other, because this part of Aunt Rosa's tale always frightened them.

'Vampees weren't attractively green and plump like us. Instead, they were bony and thin, with sunken cheeks and pale faces. Rather than magnificent buck teeth, they had horrible sharp fangs which stuck out at the edge of their cruel mouths.'

'Ugh,' Petal and Bud said together, shuddering.

'They came out only at night, when there was no moon at all. They were made very weak by moonlight and if they didn't get back to their dark, damp caves behind the waterfall before the sun rose, they died. As soon as the first rays of light struck them, they started trembling violently, fell to the ground, let out a loud,

blood-curdling scream and breathed their last.

The Vampees used to live by hunting us. When they found a victim asleep, they would pounce and smack their thin lips and utter horrible "Yum-yum" sounds throughout their cruel feast. And that was what they called us – the Yumyums.'

'That must have been so awful,' said Petal sadly. 'The worst that happens to us here is that occasionally a duck or a goose will kill one of us while it's eating the Baby's Tears we are hiding in.'

'Yes, yes, yes' said Bud impatiently, 'we all know that, so be quiet and let Aunt Rosa get to the exciting bit'. Petal 'humphed', but said no more as she didn't want to delay the story.

Collected by Kew

'One day,' continued Aunt Rosa, 'a group of men came into our warm forest. They dug up the enormous palm tree that we had lived under for as long as anyone could remember. They put the tree into a massive wooden box and filled the box with plants that lived around the base of the tree. This included a huge clump of Baby's Tears where my family and three other Plumptum families lived, and so we were put into the huge wooden plant box too.

The men filled other boxes with trees and plants. They worked all day, taking great care not to disturb the forest too much. The person in charge, Mr Quilk, said that the vegetation would quickly grow back and cover any holes they had made and so soon no one would know that they had ever been there.'

All at Sea

Aunt Rosa continued, 'We were then carried to the nearby river and the huge box I was in was put onto a boat, together with all the other boxes. From there we were taken to a very large ship, where we were stored deep inside the hold.'

She explained how the Plumptums were very frightened during the journey, but at least the families were together and there were plenty of Baby's Tears plants for them to eat.

For what seemed like an eternity but was in fact only a few weeks, they were in that ship, which went up and down, sometimes gently and sometimes with terrifying force. At first they were seasick and didn't sleep very well, but eventually they got used to the ship's motion.

Having searched the huge box they were in, they realized that there was at least one piece of good news – there were no Vampees. Sometimes Aunt Rosa thought she heard the blood-curdling sound of 'Yum-yum, Yum-yum' coming from one of the other boxes. However, because she hadn't actually seen a Vampee since they were taken from the forest, she tried to convince herself that she was just imagining things.

Mr Quilk and one or two of the other men would come down into the hold regularly to water the boxes. One day Aunt Rosa heard him explaining that the huge palm tree was going to be put into a massive see-through house of glass where it was always warm. Aunt Rosa was really looking forward to this, since the thought of always being warm again, with no Vampees to worry about, sounded like heaven.

Finally their journey was over. At the mouth of the River Thames the boxes were lifted out of the ship's hold and up into the air by crane, then they were put into a smaller boat. This boat sailed up the Thames until it reached Kew Gardens. When the boat stopped, a huge crane hook was used to lift the boxes out and onto the shore.

Catastrophe!

Without warning the weather took a serious turn for the worse, it began to pour with rain and the wind blew fiercely. The river currents picked up and quickly became very strong.

The boat rose and fell with the swell and the crane creaked under its heavy load.

Suddenly the large hook lifting the huge box containing Aunt Rosa and the other Plumptums snapped.

Shouts of horror came from the workmen as the box plummeted downwards. It crashed hard against the side of the boat and landed on the edge of the jetty. With a tremendous cracking sound the wooden box broke up, flinging its contents into the swirling river.

Luckily for Aunt Rosa, Bud, Petal and many of the other Plumtums the clump of Baby's Tears they were clinging to got stuck to a plank of wood from the box. It went careering along in the heaving, thrashing water.

Safely Ashore

The Plumptums were absolutely terrified. They sank their teeth into the wood to stop themselves from being swept away. For some time they were carried along by the roaring, fast-flowing river, but at last the plank of wood that was carrying them was washed up on the shore.

When the sun came out those who were left started to look for members of their family and friends. Luckily, most of them had survived, and they were thankful that the place where they had ended up had lots of Baby's Tears plants to eat, even if they were not as juicy as the ones in their former forest home.

The piece of wood from the original box was pulled up the bank so that it could be kept for good luck. The Plumptums felt blessed because there was no sign of any Vampees. Never again would they hear the dreadful sound of those ghouls uttering triumphant 'Yum-yums' over some poor victim.

Becoming the 'KEWtees'

Sadly, the local food had much less sap, which meant that the Plumptums' tummies would never be so plump again. Aunt Rosa was just thinking how they would soon no longer fit their Plumptum name when she noticed some writing on the piece of wood from the box that had saved them. She could make out the letters 'K E W'.

Suddenly she had a brainwave, telling the others, 'Now we're in a new place and starting a new life, let's give ourselves a new name.' She pointed to the letters and suggested, 'Let's become the Kewtees.' Everyone cheered their agreement and Aunt Rosa felt very happy, proud and really rather pleased with herself.

Since that time the Kewtees had lived safely and happily beside the Thames.

A Fishermen's Warning

Aunt Rosa believed in giving Bud and Petal freedom to roam wherever they liked, provided of course that they never left the cover of the Baby's Tears, which allowed their green-leafed heads to provide perfect camouflage.

Something Bud and Petal really enjoyed was listening to the fishermen talking on the riverbank. One day, when they had crept close to two of them, Sid and Tom, what they heard filled them with horror.

'Well, Sid, this is our last morning here on this stretch of the river. We have had some great times here, but the bulldozers are coming tomorrow to flatten this area to build new homes.'

'It's a crying shame if you ask me, Tom. All this vegetation and wildlife going to make way for houses for a few people who are rich enough to afford a view of the river.'

Bud gulped and looked at Petal, who had tears of fear welling in her eyes. 'Flatten this area … new homes,' she said in shocked disbelief. 'This is the end of our world. We must tell Aunt Rosa immediately.'

The Terrible News

Aunt Rosa made Bud and Petal repeat what they had heard three times. At first she thought it might have been a mistake, or worse – a tasteless joke. But their worried faces soon convinced her that the news was true.

Aunt Rosa thought for a moment and felt the original piece of 'K E W' wood that had brought them to safety. She always did this when she was worried about something and wanted to work out how best to respond.

'Petal, Bud,' she cried, suddenly springing into action, 'ask all the Kewtees to come to my house and we'll discuss what to do next.'

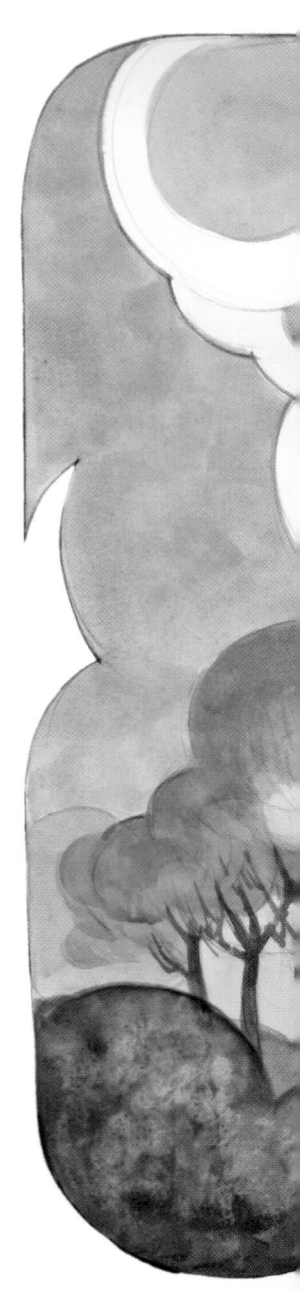

The Monster Machines

The Kewtees gathered around Aunt Rosa and the piece of the KEW box looking very miserable. They then followed her as they unhappily obeyed her demand to carry the lucky wood with them down to the relative safety of the shore.

Suddenly there were very loud engine noises and two huge bulldozers with massive open mouths roared onto the Kewtees' land. They flattened everything with their tracks and pushed the earth into big piles with their metal mouths.

Aunt Rosa, Petal, Bud and the rest of the Kewtees watched from near the shore in growing horror. The massive machines were pushing more and more earth towards them. The noise was terrible and went on all day. But just before the mounds of earth reached them, the noise stopped.

It began to rain and the miserable, frightened Kewtees huddled together. That night they found it hard to sleep. As dawn broke Aunt Rosa told them to carry the lucky wood to the very edge of the water so they could jump onto it if the earth mountain came too close. In the meantime they were to eat as much Baby's Tears as they could, in case it was some time before they found food again.

The next morning the roar of the bulldozers started up once more and the mountain of earth grew higher and higher as masses of loose earth was piled on top of it. The result was a landslide which knocked over the Kewtees and pushed the lucky plank half into the water, where it began to rise and fall in the swell.

'Quick,' shouted Aunt Rosa. 'Get onto the wood before it floats off into the Thames.'

Heron Horror

About twenty of them had just clambered on board when suddenly a big boat went past and its wash took the lucky wood out into the middle of the river. It was a nightmare journey. The plank kept afloat, but two Kewtees were swept overboard in the first minute, so Aunt Rosa shouted to everyone to bite into the wood with their buck teeth.

Then, from nowhere, a heron swooped down and landed on the wood, narrowly missing Bud, who nearly lost his grip he was so scared. But at that moment a big pleasure boat hooted its horn, frightening the heron away.

The waves behind this boat were so huge that they swept the wood that the Kewtees were clinging onto over to the opposite bank. The tide was going out and the water level was going down, so no other waves came near the wood and all the exhausted Kewtees, except for a watchful Aunt Rosa, finally fell asleep.

After a while Aunt Rosa woke Bud and Petal and asked them to climb up the bank and tell her what was on the other side.

Kew at Last

They scampered up and peered over. In front of them they could see long grass and then a path that humans were walking along. On the other side of the path was more grass, then some bushes.

They reported back to Aunt Rosa, who said, 'Right, we can't stay here because we are too exposed to passing herons, and when the tide comes in we'll be swept away into the river again.'

It had started to pour with rain. Hoping that this would mean there were no humans on the path, the Kewtees cautiously climbed the bank and crossed the path to the shelter of the grass on the other side. Aunt Rosa collapsed into her first real sleep for some time and eventually the rest of them did the same.

They awoke to find they were by a big ditch. On the other side of it was a huge park and as the sun came out they could see, glinting in the distance, a massive see-through building.

Everyone's high spirits were considerably

dampened when they discovered that the ditch separating the pathway from the big park was not only deep, it also had water in the bottom of it and seemed impassable.

Suddenly Aunt Rosa's eyes lit up. 'Cow parsley' she exclaimed. 'Look at that huge cow parsley, it has grown over the ditch and is intertwined with the bushes on the other side. It can be our bridge to Kew.'

That night they all slept soundly in some long grass, thankful and content to be in Kew. The next morning when they awoke it was a beautiful sunny day and the see-through house was shining in the distance. They set off with high hopes. Even Aunt Rosa had a bit of a spring in her step.

They made good progress over the open grass. Aunt Rosa had warned them to go round the edge, where there was long grass to protect them, but even Bud and Petal ignored her. Instead, they all headed straight across open ground towards the large glass house. Aunt Rosa didn't have enough energy left to force them to stop and just followed behind, feeling very uneasy.

Geese Attack

Without warning, her worst fears were confirmed. A flock of geese swept down and started eating their way towards the horrified Kewtees. There was no time to reach the long grass, although they moved as fast as they could. The geese were gaining on them and all seemed lost.

Suddenly two blond children started running towards the geese, shrieking gleefully as their parents chased them. Luckily, the children, their mother and heavy-footed father narrowly missed flattening the fleeing Kewtees, and best of all they scared away the geese.

Scary Squirrels

The Kewtees apologised to Aunt Rosa, but all of them were scared, exhausted and miserable. Aunt Rosa barked in exasperation, 'Take it as a sign that our future glasshouse is not in that direction. We'll follow this long grass to the right.'

They soon found drinking water and Baby's Tears and their spirits started to rise.

Next morning they saw a distant, tall, red building which the humans called the Pagoda. They began walking towards it through a pine forest, when suddenly a hail of fir cones rained down on them. One hit Bud and knocked him out. Everyone hid and soon a large grey squirrel called Spurrel came down to sniff at Bud.

They were watching in horror, when suddenly the squirrel started to sneeze. It was allergic to Kewtees.

'Let's flatten these sneeze machines by throwing things down from the trees,' shouted Spurrel. 'Stop or I'll use my magic powers, not just to make you sneeze but to turn you all to stone,' shouted Aunt Rosa.

The cowardly squirrels quickly fled from what was forever after known as Sneezing Squirrel Forest.

First Sight of the Temperate House

Life for the Kewtees settled down into a daily pattern of travelling early in the morning when there were no people about and late in the evening after the last visitors and gardeners had left.

One day Bud and Petal, who always went ahead as scouts, raced back flushed with excitement. 'Aunt Rosa,' they shouted, 'you were right of course. There is another massive see-through house.'

They all rushed forward to have a look. They cheered and lifted Aunt Rosa on their shoulders and even she was overcome. Tears of happiness rolled down her wrinkled old chubby cheeks.

'We must be careful,' she warned. 'Remember what happened with the geese.'

After two days they were within running distance of the steep grassy slope that led to the door of the see-through house.

The Kewtees dashed up the slope, across the path and crawled under the huge doors of the massive glasshouse.

They had made it.

Home at Last

Inside, the thick vegetation and huge palm trees reminded Aunt Rosa of her childhood. Tears of joy filled the eyes of all the Kewtees as they hugged each other and laughed with relief.

But in the dark, under a grating, a thin, pale-faced creature picked up a long-forgotten scent. He rushed back behind a waterfall to join five other weak creatures, telling them, 'I've smelt Yumyums. In three weeks there will be no moon and we'll go hunting.'

Meanwhile the tired but contented Kewtees were exploring their new home. Bud rushed back crying, 'I have found an enchanted forest behind a huge stairway carpeted in Baby's Tears.'

The others went to look and were so happy because it was just as Bud had described. They were in their warm, see-through home at last.

The End...